Three Little Pigs and a Gingerbread Man

For Leah and Oliver

First published in 2008
by Wayland

This paperback edition published in 2009

Reprinted in 2010 by Wayland

Text copyright © Hilary Robinson 2008
Illustration copyright © Simona Sanfilippo 2008

Wayland
338 Euston Road
London NW1 3BH

Wayland Australia
Level 17/207 Kent Street
Sydney, NSW 2000

Series Editor: Louise John
Editor: Katie Powell
Cover design: Paul Cherrill
Design: D.R.ink
Consultant: Shirley Bickler

A CIP catalogue record for this book is available from the British Library.

ISBN 9780750255189 (hbk)
ISBN 9780750255196 (pbk)

Printed in China

Wayland is a division of Hachette Children's Books,
an Hachette UK Company

www.hachette.co.uk

Three Little Pigs and a Gingerbread Man

Written by Hilary Robinson
Illustrated by Simona Sanfilippo

WAYLAND

Three little pigs lived in Pig Yard
in a house made of red bricks.

They baked all day, and had such fun,
'til a wolf began to play tricks!

He grinned and cried, "Little piggies,
it's a week since I last came to town...

...I thought I'd come and say sorry
that I blew your house of sticks down."

The wolf peered in through the window
as the three pigs mixed in a pan:
the flour, the sugar, the milk and
the eggs to bake a gingerbread man.

The pigs shut the door of the oven
and looked the wolf in the eye.

"Skedaddle!" they cried. "If we let you in, you'll turn us into pork pie!"

The wolf was now getting angry
and ran to the door round the side.

He started ringing the doorbell,
"Quick!" said the pigs. "Let's hide."

"I'll huff and I'll puff and I'll blow your house down," growled the wolf, "But I'm weary today...

...so save me the trouble and open the
door and I'll come in the easy way."

The Gingerbread Man heard all the fuss and banged on the hot oven door.

"Ready!" he cried. "I'm crispy and brown."
And he jumped down onto the floor.

"Hey, Gingerbread Man!" called the wolf with a wink. "Would you give me a hand to get in?"

"I won't let you in!" he shouted back.
"Not by the hairs on my chinny chin chin!"

The Gingerbread Man stood there fearless,
as the wolf's hunger sharpened and grew.

"Go away, you big, greedy beast! I know you'll eat me up, too!"

The wolf climbed up to the roof of the house, and looked down the chimney of bricks.

The Gingerbread Man cried, "Quick little pigs, let's light up a fire with sticks."

"That won't scare me," the mean wolf laughed, as he jumped down and looked about.

"I'll just find a bucket of water to put your silly fire out."

The wolf leapt towards the three
little pigs, as they trembled with fear
and dread.

But the Gingerbread Man came to
the rescue and kicked water all over
his head.

"Yes! Take that!" cried the Gingerbread Man, as the wolf fled from Pig Yard.

And the pigs lived happily ever after
with the Gingerbread Man as...

...their guard!

31

START READING is a series of highly enjoyable books for beginner readers. **The books have been carefully graded to match the Book Bands widely used in schools.** This enables readers to be sure they choose books that match their own reading ability.

Look out for the Band colour on the book in our Start Reading logo.

The Bands are:

Pink Band 1A & 1B

Red Band 2

Yellow Band 3

Blue Band 4

Green Band 5

Orange Band 6

Turquoise Band 7

Purple Band 8

Gold Band 9

START READING books can be read independently or shared with an adult. They promote the enjoyment of reading through satisfying stories supported by fun illustrations.

Hilary Robinson loves jumbling up stories and seeing how they turn out. Her life is a jumbled up lot of fun, too! Hilary writes books for children and produces radio programmes for BBC Radio 2 and, because she loves doing both, she really does feel as if she is living happily ever after!

Simona Sanfilippo loves to draw and paint all kinds of animals and people. She enjoyed reading illustrated fairytales as a child, and hopes you will enjoy reading these fairytale jumbles, too!